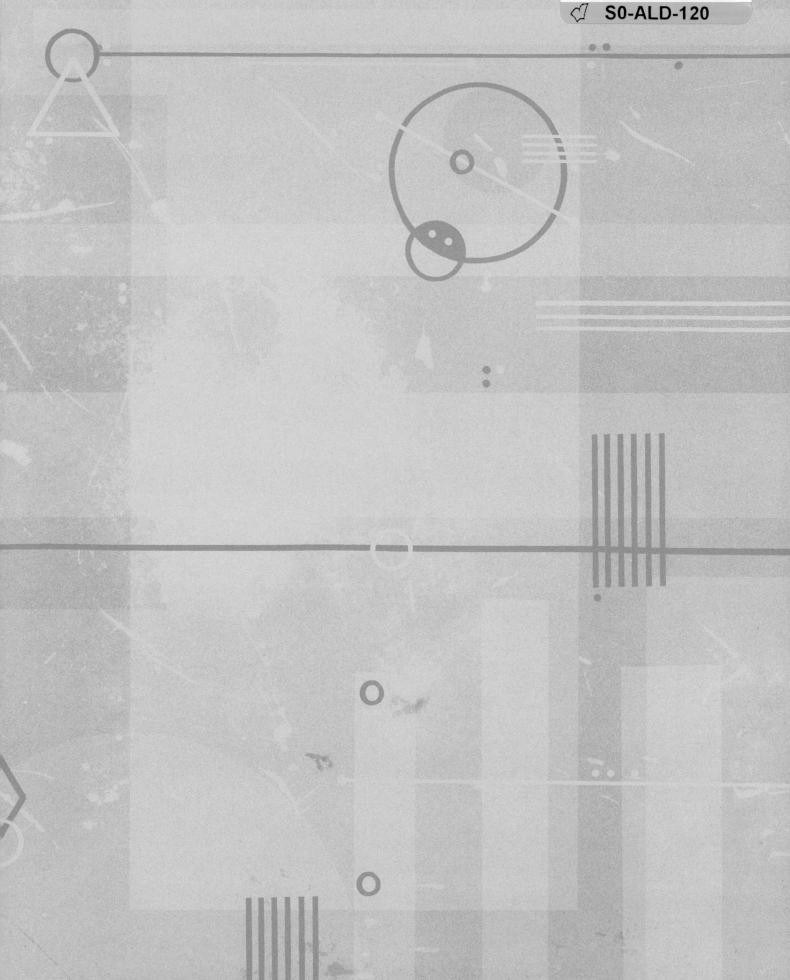

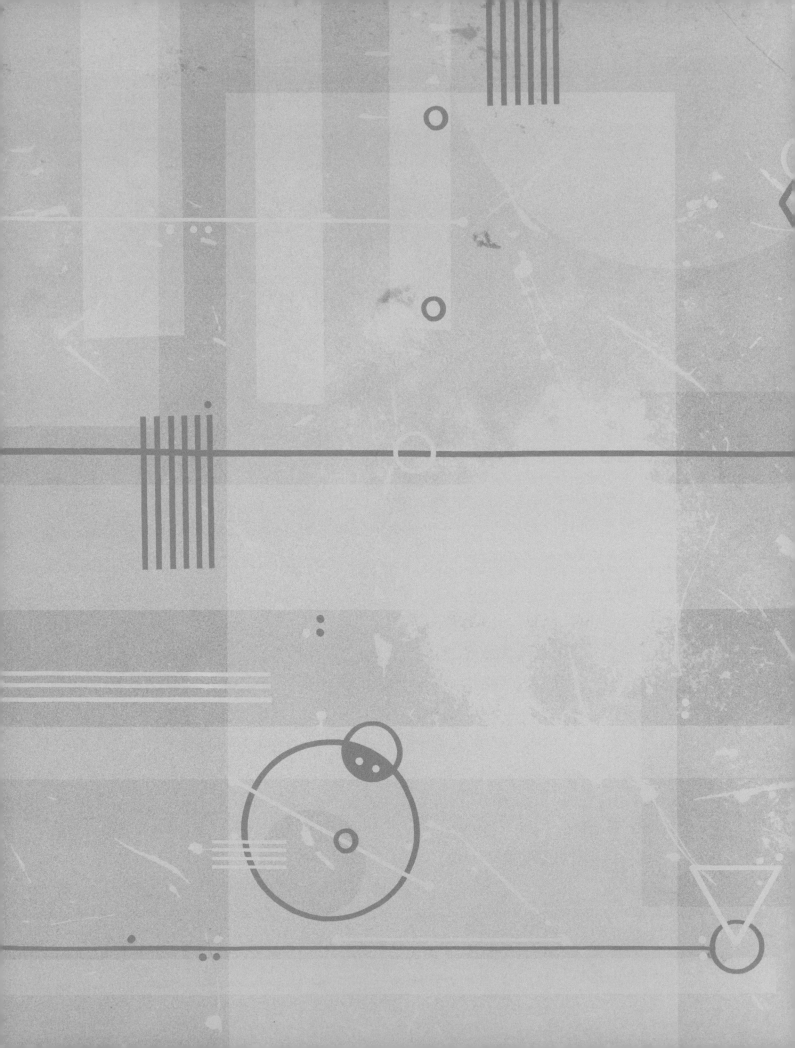

WANTS VS. NEEDS VS. ROBOTS

MICHAEL REX

Nancy Paulsen Books

For Declan and Gavin

NANCY PAULSEN BOOKS
An imprint of Penguin Random House LLC, New York

First published in the United States of America by Nancy Paulsen Books,
an imprint of Penguin Random House LLC, 2023

Visit us online at penguinrandomhouse.com.

Library of Congress Cataloging-in-Publication Data
Names: Rex, Michael, author, illustrator.
Title: Wants vs. needs vs. robots / Michael Rex.
Other titles: Wants versus needs versus robots
Description: New York: Nancy Paulsen Books, [2023] | Summary: "A group of robots demonstrates the difference between a want and a need,
by making trades to get some things they really want and accidentally giving away some things they really need"—Provided by publisher.
Identifiers: LCCN 2022020555 | ISBN 9780593530092 (hardcover) | ISBN 9780593530108 (ebook) | ISBN 9780593530115 (ebook)
Subjects: CYAC: Robots—Fiction. | Motivation (Psychology)—Fiction. | Need (Psychology)—Fiction. | Desire—Fiction. | LCGFT: Picture books.
Classification: LCC PZ7.R32875 Wan 2023 | DDC [E]—dc23
LC record available at https://lccn.loc.gov/2022020555

Manufactured in China

ISBN 9780593530092
10 9 8 7 6 5 4 3 2 1
TOPL

Edited by Nancy Paulsen
Art direction by Cecilia Yung
Design by Cindy De la Cruz
Text set in Martin Gotham URW and StupidHead BB
The art was created in Photoshop.

Do you know the difference between a

and a

WANT

NEED?

Sometimes it can be hard to tell them apart.
Even robots get them mixed up. But maybe
we can work together and figure it out.

These robots need four things.

Batteries for power.

Arms to do work.

Legs to move.

Oil so they run smoothly.

A need is something you CANNOT survive without.

Do robots need fancy sunglasses?
Do robots need jelly-bean tacos?
Do robots need unicorn hats?
Do robots need golden ukuleles?

No. They don't.
But they may want fancy sunglasses,
jelly-bean tacos, unicorn hats,
and golden ukuleles.

A want is something you do not need,
but it is something you would

ENJOY.

Sometimes we really, really, really want something so much that it feels like we need it. Let's see what happens when a robot feels like that.

Hey, that's a super-cool shirt!
I wish I had a cool shirt like that.
If I had a cool shirt like that,
I'd be the coolest!

Do you want
to trade?

But wait! Doesn't a robot need oil?
Should it trade oil for a shirt?

Would you look at
me in this cool shirt!
And hey, those are fabulous
boots! I'll trade you my
arms for those boots.

Hold on! Doesn't a robot need arms?
Should it trade away its arms?

Whoa! Its legs? Doesn't a robot need its legs? Should it give away its legs?

Not its battery! Doesn't a robot need its battery?
Should it trade away its battery?

What a mess!
See what happens when you don't
balance your wants and needs?

You end up with lots of stuff you
want, but not the things you need.

If we don't take care of our **NEEDS.**

we can't enjoy the things we **WANT.**

Let's rebuild this robot and give it another chance to figure out the difference between wants and needs.

Time for a redo! Arms! Oil! Battery! Legs!

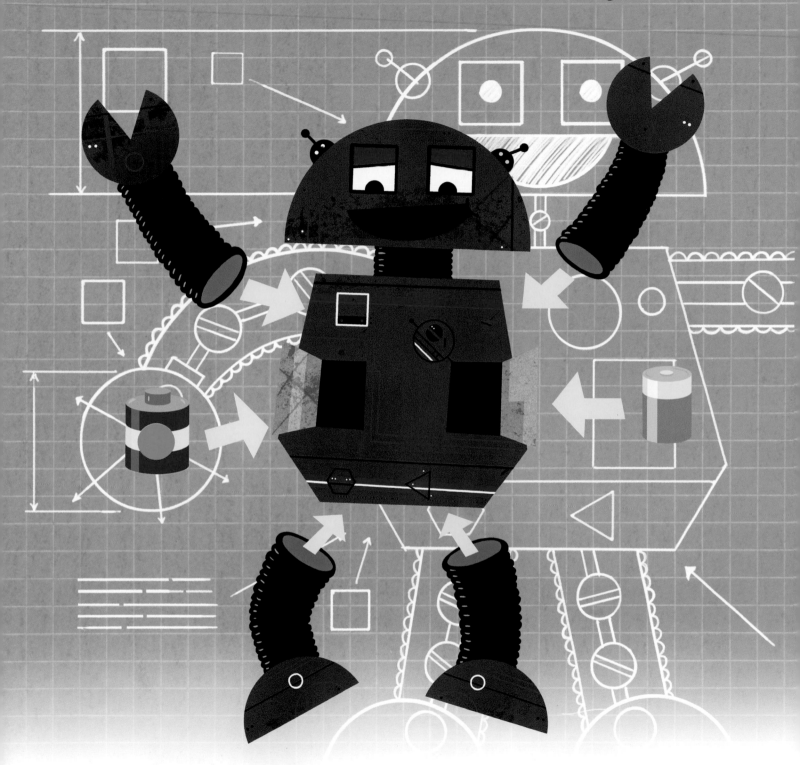

Before we go on, here's a question to think
about . . . Do you want to turn the page,
or do you need to turn the page?

Right! You want to turn the page.
You want to find out what happens next.

I need my oil.
How about I sing
you a song?

Great!
I love songs!

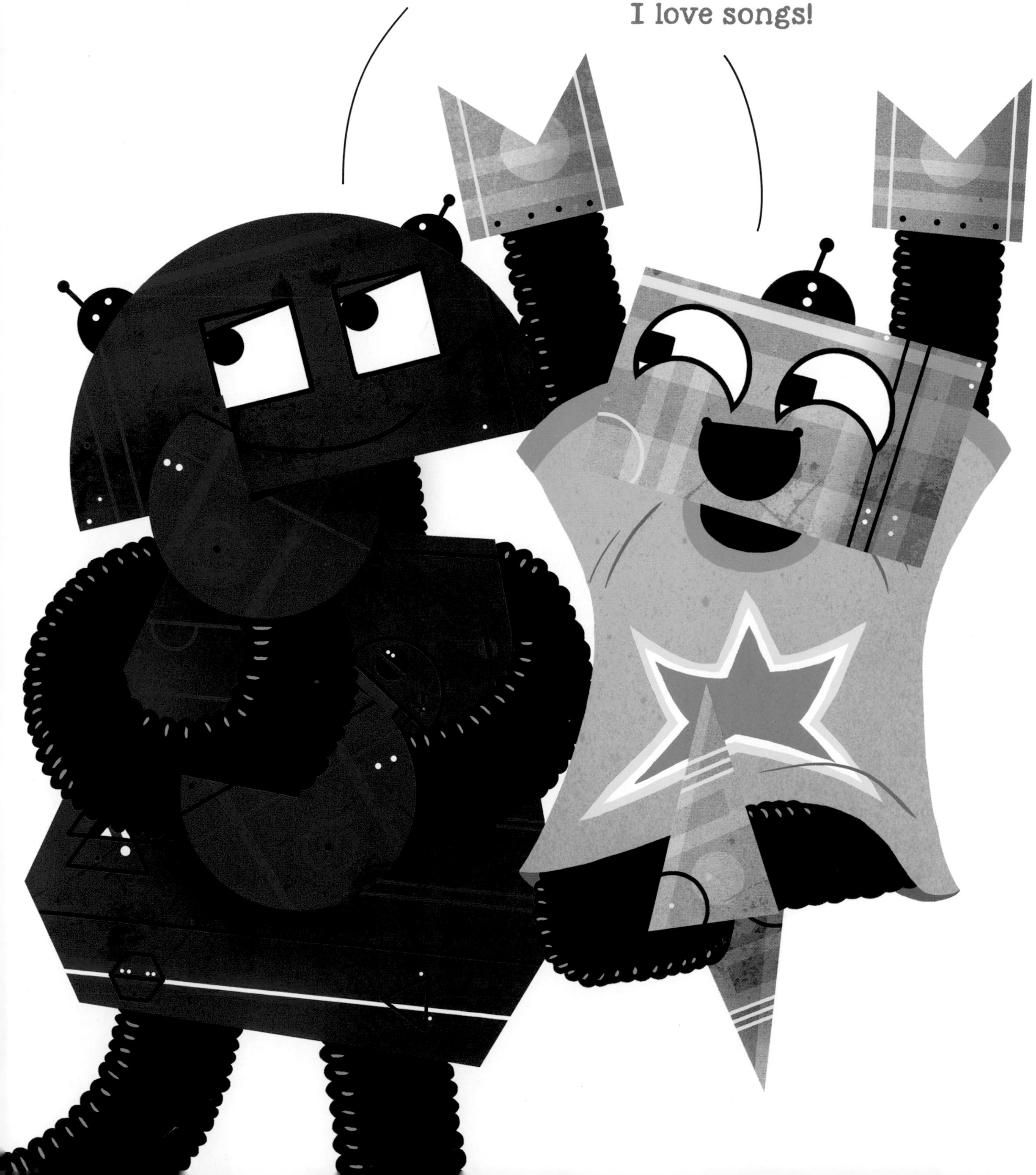

And it really was

Every day, we all have to choose between our wants and our needs.

It's okay to want things. However, we may lose interest in that awesome stuff we really, really wanted.

When that happens, it's good we
still have the things we need . . .

Oil and legs can take robots
on a long walk with good friends.

A battery and arms can give robots
the ability to build together.